To Deegan,
for finding your Cass

This Book Belongs to:

_____

DINO DEEGAN
AND THE UNPLEASANT CLASS

Written By
Heather E. Robyn

Illustrated By
Zoe Mellors

Young Deegan, he loved to play on the swings,
and soar on the playground, as though he had wings.
He played by himself, his classmates not near,
for Deegan did fill them with angst and with fear.
"Your claws are too sharp to join in our games,"
they said as they pointed and called Deegan names.
"You're creepy and odd," they yelled, and they jeered,
and poor Deegan thought, "This is just what I feared."

At home, he was sad; tears streamed down his face.
To Mom, he then asked, "Must these claws be the case?"
Mom said, "Yes, they must, my sweet Dino guy.
They're vital to do what you need to get by."
"I get that," he said. "But what should I do?
The kids at my school fear my claws through and through.
They're scared that one day, I'll give them a scrape
while playing the game 'Schoolyard Pirate Escape.'"

"That's truly a plight," Mom said, leaning in.
"But strength my young Dino, it comes from within.
You'll soon find a friend who won't be afraid,
who'll stand by your side and will come to your aid."
"Ok," Deegan said and breathed in quite deep.
"Now, dear," said his mom, "please go get some good sleep."

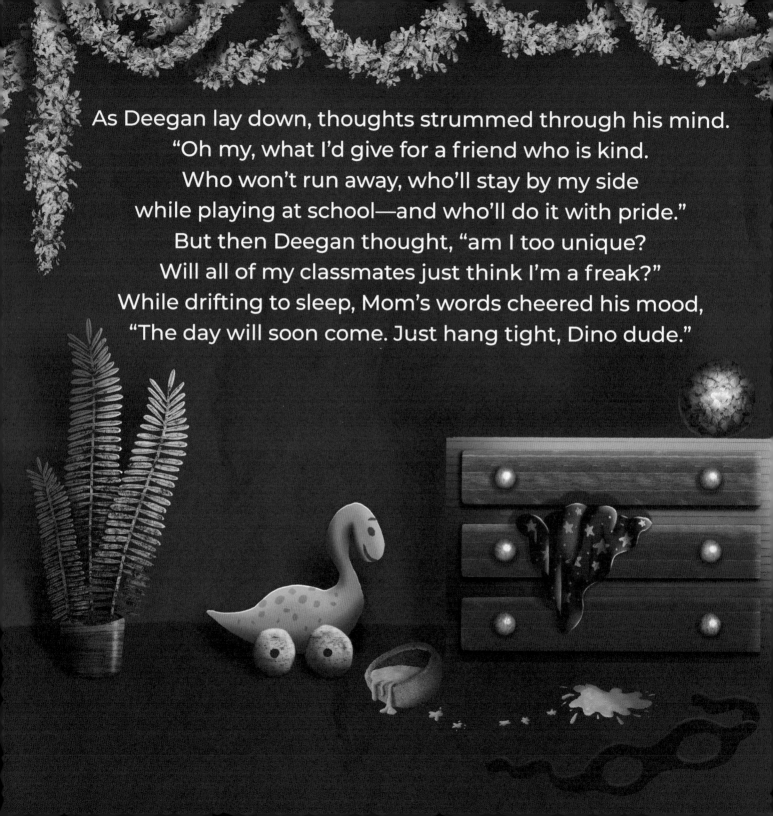

As Deegan lay down, thoughts strummed through his mind.
"Oh my, what I'd give for a friend who is kind.
Who won't run away, who'll stay by my side
while playing at school—and who'll do it with pride."
But then Deegan thought, "am I too unique?
Will all of my classmates just think I'm a freak?"
While drifting to sleep, Mom's words cheered his mood,
"The day will soon come. Just hang tight, Dino dude."

At school on the grass, he sat the next day,
observing his classmates while watching them play.
"Why don't you go play with them on the slide?"
A quiet voice asked from the red wagon ride.
"Hello," a girl said. "I'm new in the class."
While grabbing his claw, she then added, "I'm Cass."

"Be careful!" he wailed, as if by default.
"My scratches can hurt, even if no one's fault."
"No worries," said Cass, a smile on her face.
"I'm not scared at all, so let's go have a race!"

Her comforting words so warm like a fire,
they lifted his spirits up higher and higher.
But suddenly then the others chimed in,
"You must stay away; Dino scratches your skin!"

Observing her friend, the pain in his eyes,
Cass said, "What if YOU heard those words with such cries?"
They stopped, and they thought, then grasped what she said.
"You're right; they sound worse as they run through our heads.
We're sorry dear Deegan; our actions were poor.
We'll try to do better, we promise," they swore.

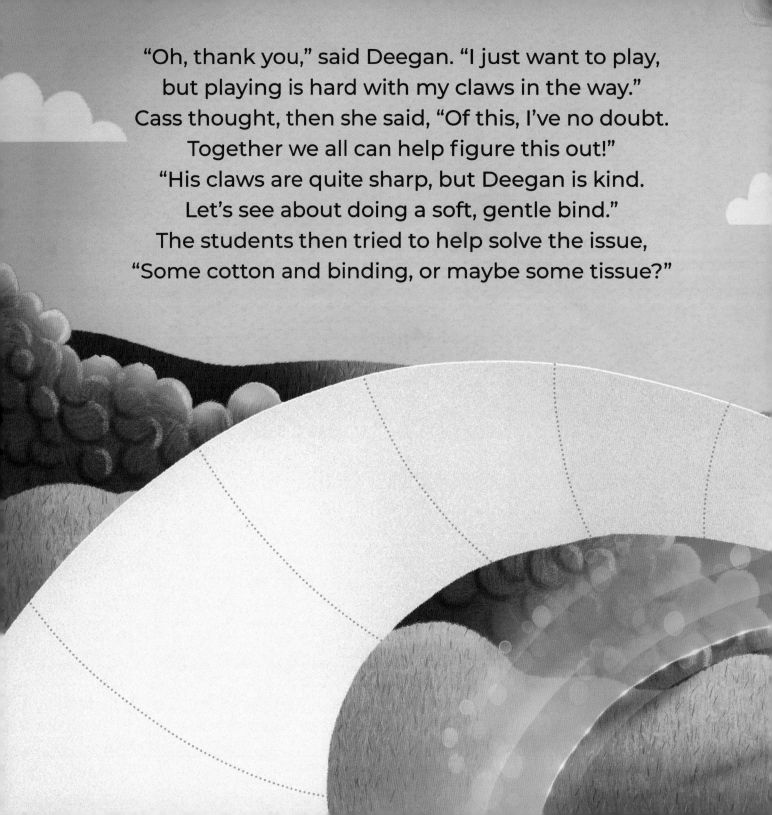

"Oh, thank you," said Deegan. "I just want to play,
but playing is hard with my claws in the way."
Cass thought, then she said, "Of this, I've no doubt.
Together we all can help figure this out!"
"His claws are quite sharp, but Deegan is kind.
Let's see about doing a soft, gentle bind."
The students then tried to help solve the issue,
"Some cotton and binding, or maybe some tissue?"

"No, wait!" cried Imani, who jumped with a spring.
"These gloves might just do it. They might be the thing!"
She gave him the gloves; his claws ripped right through,
Imani just pondered, "What else can we do?"

"I've got it," cried Angus. "Our projects with cork!"
The group's eyes all widened, "Well, that might just work!"
They grabbed all the cork and took their supply,
then crafted for him a creation to try.
"I'm nervous," said Deegan, "that nothing will work.
I'd have to miss out when you climb Mount Berzerk."
So, Angus then fastened each claw to a cushion,
ensuring that nothing was poking or pushin'.

"Let's go!" Daisy shouted, "While there is still time!"
"Come on, Dino Deegan, before the loud chime!"
They rushed to the playground and climbed Mount Berzerk.
When Deegan succeeded, he beamed a proud smirk. Then
playing some more, as he always dreamed,
he tagged all his classmates, and none of them screamed.

He ran and hugged Cass; tears filled his big eyes.
"Why, thank you, my friend, for this lovely surprise."
"My pleasure," said Cass. "I'm glad you're included.
As all should—this concept should not be disputed."

"So, what do you say? Let's finish that run.
Let's go before recess is over and done!"
They raced through the field, exuding such glee,
they both understood that true friendship is key.

Kindness Advice

"You can ask them to play with you."
Liliana, age 4

"You go up to them and introduce yourself and ask them to play and grab
their hand and lead them to the playground."
Autumn, age 6

"You ask them to come to your table and sit with them and
ask if they like to share (cookies).
Aubree, age 4

"You can help them. Show them around campus, introduce them to friends,
and exchange phone numbers."
Jeanae, age 12

"You can show kindness to others by inviting them to play with you if they are alone.
Invite them to eat lunch with you and hang out after school with them."
Jazlyn, age 10

"Just listen to what another person is saying. Not everyone does that."
Genevieve, age 13

"You can help someone when they are hurt. Show respect and listen to others."
Bailey, age 10

"If someone drops a book or anything then you can pick it up for them."
Skylar, age 7

"Be nice to them. If their balloon flies away you can share your balloon with them."
Bryce, age 5

"Give them something fun and ask if they need a friend."
Madeline, age 6

"Share something you like with them. Like toys!"
Maverick, age 4

"Say hello to a classmate you don't normally talk to, it could brighten up someone's day"
Zoe, age 29

"Invite kids to birthday parties that may not get invited to many especially if it's a big party where most of the class is being invited anyway"
Casey, age 39

"Invite the one being bullied over and include them in what I am doing."
Piper, age 11

"I would tell the bully to stop being mean and tell them it's not nice."
Jet, age 10

"Share my toys with them."
Wyatt, age 8

Meet the creative team!

About the Author

Heather was born and raised in Southern California. As an avid learner, she earned her Doctorate degree in Education and spent several years in Social Work helping foster youth and homeless veterans. She enjoys traveling with her two children and boyfriend. She resides in San Jose with her family and Husky, Echo.

For more information about Heather and her work, visit her at www.heathererobyn.com

About the Illustrator

Zoe has always had a passion for art, from sticking her hands in paint when finger painting to doodling on the margins of her school books. She studied Illustration at the University of Lincoln and wants to help tell stories like the ones that made her fall in love with art when she was being read to as a child. Zoe resides in the U.K. with her husband.

To view more of Zoe's work, visit her website at www.zoemellorsillustration.com

More by Heather E. Robyn

Super Max and the Math Menace

It was a regular school day for the students of Room 23, until the math menace arrived disguised as a surprise test ready to ruin the day! Anxiety grips Max's friends and chaos ensues because they feel unprepared to pass this test. But, Max has a little secret up her sleeve...she's super!

Super Max must help her friends overcome their test anxiety and take down the math menace one problem at a time. Will she make it in time to save the day and help her friends pass the math test?

Nearly 40% of children struggle with test anxiety. It's this anxiety that prevents them from peforming their best and can have longer affects of behavior, self esteem, and avoidance of school. Experiencing test anxiety as a child was difficult, but watching my daughter experience these symptoms influenced me to write Super Max and the Math Menace.

Super Max helps children realize their true inner power to dig deep and pull the super in themselves out to conquer fear over test anxiety. Super Max will take children and parents on an adventure of super hero discovery and the ability to help others overcome fears.

Available Now!

Printed in Great Britain
by Amazon